tha Posy

ever so nosy

Julie Fulton

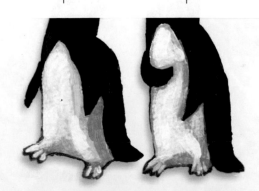

Illustrated by Jona Jung

Tabitha Posy was ever so **nosy**.
She **made** all her neighbours shout.
She'd peer round each door, ask, "WHY?" and "WHAT FOR?"
then **pester** until she found out.

"Please, leave us **alone**," they were all heard to moan,
but she grew even worse than before.
So they cried, "Get inside, draw the curtains and hide.
It's young **Tabitha**. Quick, lock your door!"

One day at her **school**, the new teacher, Miss Pool,
told the class, "We've got something **to do.**
It's a bright **sunny** day, so we'll all make our way
to see Hamilton Shady's new **ZOO."**

They first saw a **snake.** It was called Wiggly Jake
and it slithered about with great **ease.**
All **Tabitha** said as it curled round her head was,
"Do you know if snakes ever **sneeze?**"

The **owl** gave a wail when she tugged at its tail.
It flew off with a shriek to its **den**.
"I just wanted to **see** if a **feather** would be
any good back at **school** as a **pen**."

They went for a walk and heard **noisy** birds squawk,
then watched **wallabies** jumping around.
They saw **penguins** and bears, cheeky monkeys and hares,
and a **tiger** asleep on the **ground.**

It lay there and **snored,** so they all got quite bored
and **decided** to go off and **play,**
but young Tabitha said, "Look, the tiger's been fed.
What's he had for his dinner today?"

Miss Pool didn't see as she climbed up a tree,
but the **tiger** had opened an eye.
"**Ooh,** how nice; for a treat, I've been given fresh meat."
Grinned the tiger, "It's better than pie."

As Tabitha **tried** to creep up by its side,
the sly tiger began to look **mean**.

It swallowed **her** down without even a frown,
until only her **legs** could be seen.

Poor Tabitha cried as she jiggled inside
and the tiger began to feel sick.
It gave a loud moan, then a cough, then a groan,
but it **only** made Tabitha **kick.**

"I want to get **out!**" she said, wriggling about
with the feather she'd **pinched** from the **owl.**

It was tickly and **SO** the poor tiger let **go** and spat Tabitha up with a howl.

"Oh my!" said Miss Pool, "You are covered in drool and there's **spit** dripping off your wet hair. You've got mud on your dress and your face is a mess. Can we get you cleaned up anywhere?"

An **elephant's** nose made a very good hose
and the mud, spit and drool **washed** away.
As she stood there, **wet** through, soggy Tabitha knew
there was **something** she needed **to say:**

"**Please** don't make a fuss. Let's **get** back on the bus. I'm sorry," said Tabitha Posy.

"I think I should **look** for more things in a **book**, rather than being **too nosy**."

The END

Tabitha Posy was ever so Nosy
is an original concept by
© Julie Fulton

Author: Julie Fulton

Illustrator: Jona Jung
Jona Jung is represented
by MSM Studio
www.msmstudio.eu

A CIP catalogue record for this book
is available from the British Library.

**PUBLISHED BY MAVERICK ARTS
PUBLISHING LTD**

©Maverick Arts Publishing Limited (2013)
2nd Edition 2014

Studio 3A, City Business Centre,
6 Brighton Road,
Horsham,
West Sussex, RH13 5BB
+44(0) 1403 256941

ISBN 978-1-84886-097-1

Maverick
arts publishing

www.maverickbooks.co.uk

**THIS EDITION PUBLISHED
2014 FOR INDEX BOOKS**